Bliss Carman

A Winter Holiday

Bliss Carman

A Winter Holiday

ISBN/EAN: 9783337251697

Printed in Europe, USA, Canada, Australia, Japan

Cover: Foto ©Andreas Hilbeck / pixelio.de

More available books at **www.hansebooks.com**

A
WINTER HOLIDAY

BLISS CARMAN

Boston
Small, Maynard & Company
1899

THE UNIVERSITY PRESS, CAMBRIDGE, U. S. A.

Contents

Contents

A Winter Holiday

A Winter Holiday

DECEMBER IN SCITUATE

Under a hill in Scituate,
Where sleep four hundred men of Kent,
My friend one bobolincolned June
Set up his rooftree of content.

Content for not too long, of course,
Since painter's eye makes rover's heart,
And the next turning of the road
May cheapen the last touch of art.

Yet also, since the world is wide,
And noon's face never twice the same,
Why not sit down and let the sun,
That artist careless of his fame,

Exhibit to our eyes, off-hand,
As mood may dictate and time serve,
His precious, perishable scraps
Of fleeting color, melting curve?

3

A Winter Holiday

And while he shifts them all too soon,
Make vivid note of this and that,
Careful of nothing but to keep
The beauties we most marvel at.

Selective merely, bent to save
The sheer delirium of the eye,
Which best may solace or rejoice
Some fellow-rover by and by ;

That stumbling on it, he exclaim,
"What mounting sea-smoke! What a blue!"
And at the glory we beheld,
His smouldering joy may kindle too.

Merely selective ?   Bring me back,
Verbatim from the lecture hall,
Your notes of So-and-so's discourse ;
The gist and substance are not all.

The unconscious hand betrays to me
What listener it was took heed,
Eager or slovenly or prim ;
A written character indeed !

December in Scituate

Much more in painting ; every stroke
That weaves the very sunset's ply,
Luminous, palpitant, reveals
How throbbed the heart behind the eye ;

How hand was but the cunning dwarf
Of spirit, his triumphant lord
Marching in Nature's pageantry,
Elated in the vast accord.

Art is a rubric for the soul,
Man's comment on the book of earth,
The spellborn human summary
Which gives that common volume worth.

So at the pictures of my friend, —
His marginal remarks, as 't were, —
One cries not only, " What a blue ! "
But, " What a human heart beat here ! "

And now, ten minutes from the train,
Over the right-hand easy swell,
We catch the sparkle of the sea
And the green roof of Tortoise Shell.

A Winter Holiday

(He guessed from slipshod excellence
What fable to his craft applied.
The tortoise for his monitor,
And *Cur tam cito* for his guide.)

Here is the slanting open field,
Where billow upon billow rolls
The sea of daisies in the sun,
When June brings back the orioles.

All summer here the crooning winds
Are cradled in the rocking dunes,
Till they, full height and burly grown,
Go seaward and forget their croons.

And out of the Canadian north
Comes winter like a huge gray gnome,
To blanket the red dunes with snow
And muffle the green sea with foam.

I could sit here all day and watch
The seas at battle smoke and wade,
And in the cold night wake to hear
The booming of their cannonade.

December in Scituate

Then smiling turn to sleep and say,
"In vain dark's banners are unfurled;
That ceaseless roll is God's tattoo
Upon the round drum of the world."

And waking find without surprise
The first sun in a week of storm,
The southward eaves begin to drip,
And the faint Marshfield hills look warm;

The brushwood all a purple mist;
The blue sea creaming on the shore;
As if the year in his last days
Had not a sorrow to deplore.

Then evening by the fire of logs,
With some old song or some new book;
Our Lady Nicotine to share
Our single bliss; while seaward, look,—

Orion mounting peaceful guard
Over our brother's new-made tent,
Under a hill in Scituate
Where sleep so sound those men of Kent.

WINTER AT TORTOISE SHELL

"What wondrous life is this I lead !
Ripe apples drop about my head."

But as I read, that couplet seems
The merest metaphor of dreams, —

A parable from Arcady
Refuted by this wintry sea.

The summer was so long ago,
I hardly can believe it so.

Did we once really live outdoors,
With leafy walls and grassy floors,

Through sultry morns and dreamy noons
And red October in the dunes,

With butterflies and bees and things
That roamed the air on roseleaf wings ?

Winter at Tortoise Shell

There's not a leaf on any bough
To prove the truth of summer now ;

There's not an apple left on high
To bear the red sun company.

The sun himself is gone away,
A vagabond since yesterday,

And left the maniac wind to moan
Through his deserted house alone.

Over the hills we watched him forth
From the low lodges of the North ;

And then a hand we did not know
Dropped the tent-curtain of the snow.

This morning all outdoors is gray
And bleak as dead Siberia.

But what is that to lucky me ?
Who would not love captivity,

Where safe beneath their Tortoise Shell
The Lady and the Tortoise dwell ?

A Winter Holiday

The Tortoise is the Lady's son ;
He makes procrastination

A fine art in this hurrying age
Of grudging work and greedy wage.

An open air impressionist,
He swims his landscape in a mist,

And likes to paint his shadows blue,
If it is all the same to you.

If not, he does not call you blind ;
He waits for you to change your mind.

His cunning knows how color lies
Eluding the untutored eyes.

Perhaps within a year or two
You may believe his pictures true.

The Tortoise, for a pseudonym,
Is very suitable to him.

At Tortoise Shell the rafters green
Mimic a shady orchard screen,

Winter at Tortoise Shell

The kindly half-light of the leaves,
And June songs running round the eaves.

The walls are hung with tapestries
Of gold flowers bending to the breeze,

And paintings, drenched in light and sun,
Of Scituate shore and Norman town, —

A mute, unfading fairyland,
The glad work of a wizard hand, —

A small bright summer world of art
The winter cherishes at heart.

Look, through the window, where the seas,
A million strong, ride in with ease !

The mad white stallions in stampede.
This is your wintry world, indeed.

But summertime and gladness dwell
Under the roof of Tortoise Shell.

Color, imperishably fair,
Is mistress of the seasons there.

A Winter Holiday

And, ah, to-night the Gallaghers
Will come in all their mitts and furs,

Across the fields to visit us.
Then Boston *urbs* may envy *rus!*

We'll let the hooting blizzard shout;
We'll pull the little table out;

And Andrew Usher, ever blessed,
Shall comfort us beneath the vest.

So trim the light, and build the fire;
Bring out your oldest, sweetest briar.

For half an hour, if you please,
We'll listen to *The Seven Seas;*

Or Mr. Gallagher will sing —
An opera or anything —

About the Duke of Seven Dials,
About his Dolly and her wiles.

Then we will sit, but not for tea,
Around the smooth mahogany,

Winter at Tortoise Shell

And watch while houses full of kings
Are overthrown by knaves and things ;

And hear the pleasant clicking noise
Of triple-colored ivories.

And Time may learn another trick
To better his arithmetic,

When wise content subtracts a notch
For fuming weed and foaming Scotch.

To-morrow, by the early train,
Light-hearted mirth will come again

To race across-lots with a crew
Of St. Bernards, — contagious Lou.

Who would not quit, for joys like these,
All idle Southern vagrancies,

By purple cove and creamy beach,
And gold fruit hung within the reach ?

Since friendship is a thing that grows
To sturdy height in Northern snows,

A Winter Holiday

Who would not choose December weather,
Where love and cold thrive well together,

And bide his days, content to dwell
Under the eaves of Tortoise Shell?

BAHAMAN

In the crowd that thronged the pierhead,
   come to see their friends take ship
For new ventures in seafaring,
   when the hawsers were let slip
And we swung out in the current,
   with good-byes on every lip,

Midst the waving caps and kisses,
   as we dropped down with the tide
And the faces blurred and faded,
   last of all your hand I spied
Signalling, Farewell; Good fortune!
   then my heart rose up and cried,

"While the world holds one such comrade,
   whose sweet durable regard
Would so speed my safe departure,
   lest home-leaving should be hard,
What care I who keeps the ferry,
   whether Charon or Cunard!"

A Winter Holiday

Then we cleared the bar, and laid her
    on the course, the thousand miles
From the Hook to the Bahamas,
    from midwinter to the isles
Where frost never laid a finger,
    and eternal summer smiles.

Three days through the surly storm-beat,
    while the surf-heads threshed and flew,
And the rolling mountains thundered
    to the trample of the screw,
The black liner heaved and scuffled
    and strained on, as if she knew.

On the fourth, the round blue morning
    sparkled there, all light and breeze,
Clean and tenuous as a bubble
    blown from two immensities,
Shot and colored with sheer sunlight
    and the magic of those seas.

In that bright new world of wonder,
    it was life enough to laze
All day underneath the awnings,
    and through half-shut eyes to gaze
At the marvel of the sea-blue;
    and I faltered for a phrase

Bahaman

Should half give you the impression,
   tell you how the very tint
Justified your finest daring,
   as if Nature gave the hint,
" Plodders, see Imagination
   set his pallet without stint ! "

Cobalt, gobelin, and azure,
   turquoise, sapphire, indigo,
Changing from the spectral bluish
   of a shadow upon snow
To the deep of Canton china, —
   one unfathomable glow.

And the flying fish, — to see them
   in a scurry lift and flee,
Silvery as the foam they sprang from,
   fragile people of the sea,
Whom their heart's great aspiration
   for a moment had set free.

From the dim and cloudy ocean,
   thunder-centred, rosy-verged,
At the lord sun's *Sursum Corda*,
   as implicit impulse urged,
Frail as vapor, fine as music,
   these bright spirit-things emerged ;

A Winter Holiday

Like those flocks of small white snowbirds
    we have seen start up before
Our brisk walk in winter weather
    by the snowy Scituate shore;
And the tiny shining sea-folk
    brought you back to me once more.

So we ran down Abaco;
    and passing that tall sentinel
Black against the sundown, sighted,
    as the sudden twilight fell,
Nassau light; and the warm darkness
    breathed on us from breeze and swell.

Stand-by bell and stop of engine;
    clank of anchor going down;
And we're riding in the roadstead
    off a twinkling-lighted town,
Low dark shore with boom of breakers
    and white beach the palm-trees crown.

In the soft wash of the sea air,
    on the long swing of the tide,
Here for once the dream came true,
    the voyage ended close beside
The Hesperides in moonlight
    on mid-ocean where they ride.

And those Hesperidian joy-lands
    were not strange to you and me.
Just beyond the lost horizon,
    every time we looked to sea
From Testudo, there they floated,
    looming plain as plain could be.

Who believed us ?   " Myth and fable
    are a science in our time."
" Never saw the sea that color."
    " Never heard of such a rhyme."
Well, we've proved it, prince of idlers, —
    knowledge wrong and faith sublime.

Right were you to follow fancy,
    give the vaguer instinct room
In a heaven of clear color,
    Where the spirit might assume
All her elemental beauty,
    past the fact of sky or bloom.

Paint the vision, not the view, —
    the touch that bids the sense good-bye,
Lifting spirit at a bound
    beyond the frontiers of the eye,
To suburb unguessed dominions
    of the soul's credulity.

A Winter Holiday

Never yet was painter, poet,
    born content with things that are, —
Must divine from every beauty
    other beauties greater far,
Till the arc of truth be circled,
    and her lantern blaze, a star.

This alone is art's ambition,
    to arrest with form and hue
Dominant ungrasped ideals,
    known to credence, hid from view,
In a mimic of creation, —
    To the life, yet fairer too, —

Where the soul may take her pleasure,
    contemplate perfection's plan,
And returning bring the tidings
    of his heritage to man, —
News of continents uncharted
    she has stood tiptoe to scan.

So she fires his gorgeous fancy
    with a cadence, with a line,
Till the artist wakes within him,
    and the toiler grows divine,
Shaping the rough world about him
    nearer to some fair design.

Bahaman

Every heart must have its Indies, —
    an inheritance unclaimed
In the unsubstantial treasure
    of a province never named,
Loved and longed for through a lifetime,
    dull, laborious, and unfamed,

Never wholly disillusioned.
    Spiritus, read, *hæres sit*
Patriæ quæ tristia nescit.
    This alone the great king writ
O'er the tomb of her he cherished
    in this fair world she must quit.

Love in one farewell forever,
    taking counsel to implore
Best of human benedictions
    on its dead, could ask no more.
The heart's country for a dwelling,
    this at last is all our lore.

But the fairies at your cradle
    gave you craft to build a home
In the wide bright world of color,
    with the cunning of a gnome ;
Blessed you so above your fellows
    of the tribe that still must roam.

A Winter Holiday

Still across the world they go,
    tormented by a strange unrest,
And the unabiding spirit
    knocks forever at their breast,
Bidding them away to fortune
    in some undiscovered West ;

While at home you sit and call
    the Orient up at your command,
Master of the iris seas
    and Prospero of the purple land.
Listen, here was one world-corner
    matched the cunning of your hand.

Not, my friend, since we were children,
    and all wonder-tales were true, —
Jason, Hengest, Hiawatha,
    fairy prince or pirate crew, —
Was there ever such a landing
    in a country strange and new

Up the harbor where there gathered,
    fought and revelled many a year,
Swarthy Spaniard, lost Lucayan,
    Loyalist, and Buccaneer,
" Once upon a time " was now,
    and " far across the sea " was here.

Bahaman

Tropic moonlight, in great floods
  and fathoms pouring through the trees
On a ground as white as sea-froth
  its fantastic traceries,
While the poincianas, rustling
  like the rain, moved in the breeze,

Showed a city, coral-streeted,
  melting in the mellow shine,
Built of creamstone and enchantment,
  fairy work in every line,
In a velvet atmosphere
  that bids the heart her haste resign.

Thanks to Julian Hospitator,
  saint of travellers by sea,
Roving minstrels and all boatmen, —
  just such vagabonds as we, —
On the shaded wharf we landed,
  rich in leisure, hale and free.

What more would you for God's creatures,
  but the little tide of sleep ?
In a clean white room I wakened,
  saw the careless sunlight peep
Through the roses at the window,
  lay and listened to the creep

A Winter Holiday

Of the soft wind in the shutters,
  heard the palm-tops stirring high,
And that strange mysterious shuffle
  of the slipshod foot go by.
In a world all glad with color,
  gladdest of all things was I ;

In a quiet convent garden,
  tranquil as the day is long,
Here to sit without intrusion
  of the world or strife or wrong, —
Watch the lizards chase each other,
  and the green bird make his song ;

Warmed and freshened, lulled yet quickened
  in that Paradisal air,
Motherly and uncapricious,
  healing every hurt or care,
Wooing body, mind, and spirit
  firmly back to strong and fair ;

By the Angelus reminded,
  silence waits the touch of sound,
As the soul waits her awaking
  to some *Gloria* profound;
Till the mighty Southern Cross
  is lighted at the day's last bound.

And if ever your fair fortune
   make you good Saint Vincent's guest,
At his door take leave of trouble,
   welcomed to his decent rest,
Of his ordered peace partaker,
   by his solace healed and blessed;

Where this flowered cloister garden,
   hidden from the passing view,
Lies behind its yellow walls
   in prayer the holy hours through ;
And beyond, that fairy harbor,
   floored in malachite and blue.

In that old white-streeted city
   gladness has her way at last ;
Under burdens finely poised,
   and with a freedom unsurpassed,
Move the naked-footed bearers
   in the blue day deep and vast.

This is Bay Street broad and low-built,
   basking in its quiet trade ;
Here the sponging fleet is anchored ;
   here shell trinkets are displayed ;
Here the cable news is posted daily ;
   here the market 's made,

A Winter Holiday

With its oranges from Andros,
    heaps of yam and tamarind,
Red-juiced shadducks from the Current,
    ripened in the long trade-wind,
Gaudy fish from their sea-gardens,
    yellow-tailed and azure-finned.

Here a group of diving boys
    in bronze and ivory, bright and slim,
Sparkling copper in the high noon,
    dripping loin-cloth, polished limb,
Poised a moment and then plunged
    in that deep daylight green and dim.

Here the great rich Spanish laurels
    spread across the public square
Their dense solemn shade; and near by,
    half within the open glare,
Mannerly in their clean cottons,
    knots of blacks are waiting there

By the court-house, where a magistrate
    is hearing cases through,
Dealing justice prompt and level,
    as the sturdy English do, —
One more tent-peg of the Empire,
    holding that great shelter true.

Bahaman

Last the picture from the town's end,
   palmed and foam-fringed through the cane,
Where the gorgeous sunset yellows
   pour aloft and spill and stain
The pure amethystine sea
   and far faint islands of the main.

Loveliest of the Lucayas,
   peace be yours till time be done!
In the gray North I shall see you,
   with your white streets in the sun,
Old pink walls and purple gateways,
   where the lizards bask and run,

Where the great hibiscus blossoms
   in their scarlet loll and glow,
And the idling gay bandannas
   through the hot noons come and go,
While the ever stirring sea-wind
   sways the palm-tops to and fro.

Far from stress and storm forever,
   dream behind your jalousies,
While the long white lines of breakers
   crumble on your reefs and keys,
And the crimson oleanders
   burn against the peacock seas.

FLYING FISH

WHERE the Southern liners go,
In the push of the purple seas,
When sky and ocean merge
Their blue immensities,

A creature novel and fine
Will break from the foam and play,
Swift as a leaf on the wind,
Part of the light and spray.

Will scud like a gust of snow,
Silver diaphanous things,
As if, when the sun gave will,
The sea for his part gave wings.

For æons the Titan deep
Forged and fashioned and framed,
In the great water-mills,
Forms that no man has named.

Flying Fish

With hammer of thunderous seas,
With smooth attrition of tides,
Shaping each joint and valve,
Putting the heart in their sides,

Blindly he labored and slow,
With patience ungrudging and vast,
Moulding the marvels he wrought
Nearer some purpose at last.

Not his own.   Those creatures of his
Were endowed with an alien spark,
And a hint of groping mind
That made for an unseen mark.

For part was the stroke of force,
Fortuitous, blind, and fell,
And part was the breath of soul
Inhabiting film and cell.

Finer and frailer they grew;
Must dare and be glad and aspire,
Out of the nether gloom
Into the pale sea-fire,

Out of the pale sea-day
Into the sparkle and air,

A Winter Holiday

Quitting the elder home
For the venture bright and rare.

Ah, Silver-fin, you too
Must follow the faint ahoy
Over the welter of life
To radiant moments of joy !

IN BAY STREET

" What do you sell, John Camplejohn,
   In Bay Street by the sea ? "
" Oh, turtle shell is what I sell,
   In great variety :

" Trinkets and combs and rosaries,
   All keepsakes from the sea ;
   'T is choose and buy what takes the eye,
   In such a treasury."

" 'T is none of these, John Camplejohn,
   Though curious they be,
   But something more I 'm looking for,
   In Bay Street by the sea.

" Where can I buy the magic charm
   Of the Bahaman sea,
   That fills mankind with peace of mind
   And soul's felicity ?

3   31

A Winter Holiday

"Now, what do you sell, John Cample-
       john,
  In Bay Street by the sea,
  Tinged with that true and native blue
  Of lapis lazuli ?

"Look from your door, and tell me now
  The color of the sea.
  Where can I buy that wondrous dye,
  And take it home with me ?

"And where can I buy that rustling sound,
  In this city by the sea,
  Of the plumy palms in their high blue
      calms ;
  Or the stately poise and free

"Of the bearers who go up and down,
  Silent as mystery,
  Burden on head, with naked tread,
  In the white streets by the sea ?

"And where can I buy, John Cample-
      john,
  In Bay Street by the sea,
  The sunlight's fall on the old pink wall,
  Or the gold of the orange-tree ?"

In Bay Street

" Ah, that is more than I 've heard tell
    In Bay Street by the sea,
    Since I began, my roving man,
    A trafficker to be.

" As sure as I 'm John Camplejohn,
    And Bay Street 's by the sea,
    Those things for gold have not been sold,
    Within my memory.

" But what would you give, my roving
        man
    From countries over-sea,
    For the things you name, the life of the
        same,
    And the power to bid them be ? "

" I 'd give my hand, John Camplejohn,
    In Bay Street by the sea,
    For the smallest dower of that dear power
    To paint the things I see."

" My roving man, I never heard,
    On any land or sea
    Under the sun, of any one
    Could sell that power to thee."

" 'T is sorry news, John Camplejohn,
 If this be destiny,
 That every mart should know that art,
 Yet none can sell it me.

" But look you, here 's the grace of God :
 There 's neither price nor fee,
 Duty nor toll, that can control
 The power to love and see.

" To each his luck, John Camplejohn,
 Say I.   And as for me,
 Give me the pay of an idle day
 In Bay Street by the sea.''

MIGRANTS

HELLO, whom have we here
Under the orange-trees,
Where the old convent wall
Looks to the turquoise seas?

In his jacket of olive green
He slips from bough to bough,
With a familiar air
No venue could disavow.

Good-day to you, quiet sir!
We have been friends before,
When lilacs were in bloom
By the lovely Scituate shore.

When the surly hordes of snow
Came down on the trains of the wind,
Two sojourners, it seems,
Were of a single mind.

35

A Winter Holiday

Both from the storm and gray,
The stress of the northern year,
Seeking the peace of the world,
Found tranquillity here.

Here where there is no haste,
Lead we, each in his way,
Undistracted a while,
The slow sweet life of a day.

Busy, contented, and shy,
Through the green shade you go ;
So unobtrusive and fair
A mien few mortals know.

It needs not the task be hard,
Nor the achievement sublime,
If only the soul be great,
Free from the fever of time.

And your glad being confirms
The ancient *Bonum est*
Nos hic esse of earth,
With serene, unanxious zest,

Migrants

Whether far North you fare,
When too brief spring once more
Visits the stone-walled fields
Beside the Scituate shore,

Or here in an endless June
Under the orange-trees,
Where the old convent wall
Looks to the turquoise seas.

WHITE NASSAU

THERE is fog upon the river, there is mirk
    upon the town;
You can hear the groping ferries as they hoot
    each other down;
From the Battery to Harlem there's seven
    miles of slush,
Through looming granite canyons of glitter,
    noise, and rush.

Are you sick of phones and tickers and
    crazing cable gongs,
Of the theatres, the hansoms, and the breath-
    less Broadway throngs,
Of Flouret's and the Waldorf and the chilly,
    drizzly Park,
When there's hardly any morning and five
    o'clock is dark?

I know where there's a city, whose streets
    are white and clean,
And sea-blue morning loiters by walls where
    roses lean,

White Nassau

And quiet dwells; that's Nassau, beside her
    creaming key,
The queen of the Lucayas in the blue Baha-
    man sea.

She's ringed with surf and coral, she's
    crowned with sun and palm;
She has the old-world leisure, the regal
    tropic calm;
The trade winds fan her forehead; in ever-
    lasting June
She reigns from deep verandas above her
    blue lagoon.

She has had many suitors,— Spaniard and
    Buccaneer, —
Who roistered for her beauty and spilt their
    blood for her;
But none has dared molest her, since the
    Loyalist Deveaux
Went down from Carolina a hundred years
    ago.

Unmodern, undistracted, by grassy ramp
    and fort,
In decency and order she holds her modest
    court;

She seems to have forgotten rapine and greed
    and strife,
In that unaging gladness and dignity of life.

Through streets as smooth as asphalt and
    white as bleaching shell,
Where the slip-shod heel is happy and the
    naked foot goes well,
In their gaudy cotton kerchiefs, with sway-
    ing hips and free,
Go her black folk in the morning to the
    market of the sea.

Into her bright sea-gardens the flushing tide-
    gates lead,
Where fins of chrome and scarlet loll in the
    lifting weed ;
With the long sea-draft behind them, through
    luring coral groves
The shiny water-people go by in painted
    droves.

Under her old pink gateways, where Time
    a moment turns,
Where hang the orange lanterns and the red
    hibiscus burns,

Live the harmless merry lizards, quicksilver
    in the sun,
Or still as any image with their shadow on
    a stone.

Through the lemon-trees at leisure a tiny
    olive bird
Moves all day long and utters his wise as-
    suring word ;
While up in their blue chantry murmur the
    solemn palms,
At their litanies of joyance, their ancient
    ceaseless psalms.

There in the endless sunlight, within the
    surf's low sound,
Peace tarries for a lifetime at doorways un-
    renowned ;
And a velvet air goes breathing across the
    sea-girt land,
Till the sense begins to waken and the soul
    to understand.

There's a pier in the East River, where a
    black Ward Liner lies,
With her wheezy donkey-engines taking
    cargo and supplies ;

A Winter Holiday

She will clear the Hook to-morrow for the
    Indies of the West,
For the lovely white girl city in the Islands
    of the Blest.

She 'll front the riding winter on the gray
    Atlantic seas,
And thunder through the surf-heads till her
    funnels crust and freeze ;
She 'll grapple the Southeaster, the Thing
    without a Mind,
Till she drops him, mad and monstrous,
    with the light ship far behind.

Then out into a morning all summer warmth
    and blue !
By the breathing of her pistons, by the pur-
    ring of the screw,
By the springy dip and tremor as she rises,
    you can tell
Her heart is light and easy as she meets
    the lazy swell.

With the flying fish before her, and the
    white wake running aft,
Her smoke-wreath hanging idle, without
    breeze enough for draft,

White Nassau

She will travel fair and steady, and in the
  afternoon
Run down the floating palm-tops where lift
  the Isles of June.

With the low boom of breakers for her only
  signal gun,
She will anchor off the harbor when her
  thousand miles are done,
And there's my love, white Nassau, girt
  with her foaming key,
The queen of the Lucayas in the blue
  Bahaman sea !

This first edition of A WINTER HOLIDAY *is printed for Small, Maynard & Company at The University Press in Cambridge, U. S. A., November, 1899*

www.ingramcontent.com/pod-product-compliance
Lightning Source LLC
Chambersburg PA
CBHW030903260626
47169CB00008B/2670